RIDDLE-ME RHYMES

Selected by MYRA COHN LIVINGSTON
illustrated by REBECCA PERRY

MARGARET K. McELDERRY BOOKS
New York

Maxwell Macmillan Canada
Toronto

Maxwell Macmillan International
New York   Oxford   Singapore   Sydney

FOR ERIC AND PARKER
ANDREW AND KEVIN

Margaret K. McElderry Books
Macmillan Publishing Company
866 Third Avenue
New York, NY 10022

Maxwell Macmillan Canada, Inc.
1200 Eglinton Avenue East
Suite 200
Don Mills, Ontario M3C 3N1

Macmillan Publishing Company is part of the Maxwell Communication Group
of Companies.
First edition
Printed in the United States of America
10 9 8 7 6 5 4 3 2 1
The text of this book is set in 11 pt. Palatino.
The illustrations are rendered in pen and ink.

Library of Congress Cataloging-in-Publication Data
Riddle-me rhymes / selected by Myra Cohn Livingston. — 1st ed.
        p.   cm.
    Includes index.
    ISBN 0-689-50602-3
    1. Riddles, Juvenile.   [1. Riddles.   2. Poetry—Collections.]
I. Livingston, Myra Cohn.   II. Title: Riddle me rhymes.
PN6371.5.R53   1994
398.6—dc20   93-25179

ACKNOWLEDGMENTS

The editor and publisher thank the following for permission to reprint the copyrighted material listed below. Every effort has been made to locate all persons having any rights or interests in the material published here. Any existing rights not here acknowledged will, if the editor or publisher is notified, be duly acknowledged in future editions of this book.

A. R. Beal, literary executor of the James Reeves Estate, for "Spells," from *Complete Poems for Children* by James Reeves.

Boyds Mills Press for "Look me straight in the eye . . ." and "Tall and thin and topped with a T" by William Jay Smith. From *Behind the King's Kitchen: A Roster of Riddles* compiled by William Jay Smith and Carol Ra. Copyright © 1992 by William Jay Smith and Carol Ra. Reprinted by permission of Wordsong, Boyds Mills Press, Inc. All rights reserved.

Estate of Sylvia Cassedy for "Who Am I?"; "Who Was It?"; "Who?"; and "A Riddle" by Sylvia Cassedy. From *Moon-Uncle, Moon-Uncle: Rhymes from India*, selected and translated by Sylvia Cassedy and Parvathi Thampi, Doubleday & Co., Inc., Garden City, NY, 1973. Copyright © 1973 by Sylvia Cassedy. By permission of Ellen Cassedy.

The Ciardi family for "I Met a Man That Was All Head" and "This Man Lives at My House Now," from *I Met a Man* by John Ciardi, Houghton Mifflin Co. Copyright © 1961 by John Ciardi. "Riddle," from *Fast and Slow* by John Ciardi, Houghton Mifflin Co. Copyright © 1975 by John Ciardi.

Curtis Brown Ltd. for "Mingled Yarns," from *One Winter Night in August* by X. J. Kennedy. Copyright © 1975 by X. J. Kennedy. Reprinted by permission of Curtis Brown Ltd.

Robert Froman for "Puzzle," from *Street Poems* by Robert Froman. Copyright © 1971 by Robert Froman.

Harcourt Brace & Company for "Rat Riddles," from *Good Morning, America*, copyright © 1928 and renewed 1956 by Carl Sandburg, reprinted by permission of Harcourt Brace & Company.

HarperCollins Publishers for "Alive without breath," "This thing all things devours," and "Voiceless it cries" by J. R. R. Tolkien. From *The Hobbit* by J. R. R. Tolkien. Reprinted by permission of George Allen & Unwin, now Unwin Hyman, an imprint of HarperCollins Publishers Limited.

Henry Holt and Company, Inc. for "One Guess," from *The Poetry of Robert Frost* edited by Edward Connery Lathem. Copyright © 1936 by Robert Frost. Copyright © 1964 by Lesley Frost Ballantine. Copyright © 1969 by Henry Holt and Company, Inc. Reprinted by permission of Henry Holt and Company, Inc.

Houghton Mifflin Company for "Alive without breath," "This thing all things devours," and "Voiceless it cries" by J. R. R. Tolkien. From *The Hobbit* by J. R. R. Tolkien. Copyright © 1965 by J. R. R. Tolkien. "I come more softly than a bird" and "I never speak a word" by Mary Austin. From *The Children Sing in the Far West* by Mary Austin. Copyright © 1928 by Mary Austin. Copyright © renewed 1956 by Kenneth M. Chapman and Mary C. Wheelwright. Reprinted by permission of Houghton Mifflin Company. All rights reserved.

J. Patrick Lewis for "To folks in Maine," "What's in a song, but not in a tune," and "Which tree can hang," copyright © 1994 by J. Patrick Lewis.

Little, Brown and Company for "A narrow Fellow in the Grass," "An everywhere of silver," and "Drab habitation of whom?" by Emily Dickinson. From *The Complete Poems of Emily Dickinson* edited by Thomas H. Johnson. Copyright © 1929 by Martha Dickinson Bianchi. Copyright © renewed 1957 by Mary L. Hampson. "Riddle-Me Rhyme" by David McCord. From *Speak Up* by David McCord. Copyright © 1979, 1980 by David McCord. All selections reprinted by permission of Little, Brown and Company.

George Macbeth for excerpt from "A Riddle." From *The Night of Stones*, Atheneum. Copyright © 1968 by George Macbeth.

Macmillan Publishing Company for "Living Tenderly" and #'s 2 and 3, from "Seven Natural Songs" by May Swenson. Reprinted with permission of Macmillan Publishing Company from *The Complete Poems to Solve* by May Swenson. Copyright © 1993 by The Literary Estate of May Swenson.

The Putnam Publishing Group for "What am I?" by Dorothy Aldis. Reprinted by permission of G. P. Putnam's Sons from *Hop, Skip and Jump!*, copyright © 1943 by Dorothy Aldis. Copyright © renewed 1971 by Roy E. Porter.

Marian Reiner for "Who Cast My Shadow?" from *Think of Shadows* by Lilian Moore. Copyright © 1975, 1980 by Lilian Moore. Reprinted by permission of Marian Reiner for the author. "I'm banged and chopped and sliced" and "A worthless article," from *Who Would Marry a Mineral?* by Lillian Morrison. Copyright © 1978 by Lillian Morrison. Reprinted by permission of Marian Reiner for the author. "Something's in my pocket," from *Blackberry Ink* by Eve Merriam. Copyright © 1985 by Eve Merriam. "It Isn't," from *A Word or Two With You* by Eve Merriam. Copyright © 1981 by Eve Merriam. "Riddle-Go-Round," from *Out Loud* by Eve Merriam. Copyright © 1973 by Eve Merriam. All three selections reprinted by permission of Marian Reiner for the author. "Riddle" and "Five Scottish Riddle Rhymes" by Myra Cohn Livingston. Copyright © 1994 by Myra Cohn Livingston. Used by permission of Marian Reiner for the author.

Alice Schertle for "The Prisoner." Copyright by Alice Schertle.

Ian Serraillier for "Riddle." Copyright by Ian Serraillier.

Brian Swann for "When" and "Whose." Copyright by Brian Swann.

Anita Wintz for "Solo, you go." Copyright © 1994 by Anita Wintz.

CONTENTS

I. Alive, Alive, Oh!

ONE GUESS

He has dust in his eyes and a fan for a wing,
A leg akimbo with which he can sing,
And a mouthful of dye stuff instead of a sting.

Robert Frost

a grasshopper.

4

A RIDDLE

With a million pennies
on a golden fan,
who is richer
than the richest man?

Riddle from India
translated by Sylvia Cassedy

a peacock

Alive without breath,
As cold as death;
Never thirsty, ever drinking,
All in mail never clinking.

J. R. R. Tolkien

Four diddle-diddle-danders
Two stiff-stiff-standers
Two lookers
Two hookers
And a swishabout.

Anonymous

a cow

As black as ink and isn't ink,
As white as milk and isn't milk,
As soft as silk and isn't silk,
And hops about like a filly-foal.

Anonymous

a magpie

FROM THROUGH THE LOOKING-GLASS AND WHAT ALICE FOUND THERE

"First, the fish must be caught."
That is easy: a baby, I think, could have caught it.
"Next, the fish must be bought."
That is easy: a penny, I think, would have bought it.

"Now cook me the fish!"
That is easy, and will not take more than a minute.
"Let it lie in a dish!"
That is easy, because it already is in it.

"Bring it here! Let me sup!"
It is easy to set such a dish on the table.
"Take the dish-cover up!"
Ah, *that* is so hard that I fear I'm unable!

For it holds it like glue—
Holds the lid to the dish, while it lies in the middle:
Which is easiest to do,
Un-dish-cover the fish, or dishcover the riddle?

Answer:

Get an oyster-knife strong,
Insert it 'twixt cover and dish in the middle;
Then you shall before long
Un-dish-cover the OYSTERS—dishcover the riddle!

Lewis Carroll

WHO WAS IT?

Who was it came in the dead of the night,
padding as softly as the pale moonlight?
Who was it came when the night was still?
Who broke the bowl on the windowsill?
Who was it came under darkened skies,
with greed in his heart and bulbs in his eyes?
I know who it was and so do you;
I know who it was, but I won't tell who.

Riddle from India
translated by Sylvia Cassedy

WHEN

When I'm on your lawn
you all go quiet
hoping to catch me

I am listening
though still

When you get too close
I take off
stretching myself out
to twice my length

Don't follow or
if you do

prepare to shrink
and tumble to strange dark

Brian Swann

a rabbit

LIVING TENDERLY

My body a rounded stone
with a pattern of smooth seams.
My head a short snake,
retractive, projective.
My legs come out of their sleeves
or shrink within,
and so does my chin.
My eyelids are quick clamps.

My back is my roof.
I am always at home.
I travel where my house walks.
It is a smooth stone.
It floats within the lake,
or rests in the dust.
My flesh lives tenderly
inside its bone.

May Swenson

a turtle

A narrow Fellow in the Grass
Occasionally rides—
You may have met Him—did you not
His notice sudden is—

The Grass divides as with a Comb—
A spotted shaft is seen—
And then it closes at your feet
And opens further on—

He likes a Boggy Acre
A Floor too cool for Corn—
Yet when a Boy, and Barefoot—
I more than once at Noon
Have passed, I thought, a Whip lash
Unbraiding in the Sun
When stooping to secure it
It wrinkled, and was gone—

Several of Nature's People
I know, and they know me—
I feel for them a transport
Of cordiality—

But never met this Fellow
Attended, or alone
Without a tighter breathing
And Zero at the Bone—

Emily Dickinson

a snake

RIDDLE-ME RHYME

Riddle-me, Riddle-me, Ree,
An owl is in that tree.
Riddle-me, Riddle-me, Ro,
He's there and he won't go.
Riddle-me, Riddle-me, Ree,
"I'm staying here," says he.
Riddle-me, Riddle-me, Ro,
"Caw-caw," caws the crow.
Riddle-me, Riddle-me, Ree,
An owl by day can't see.
Riddle-me, Riddle-me, Ro,
But he can hear the crow.
Riddle-me, Riddle-me, Ree,
Not *one* crow: now but three.
Riddle-me, Riddle-me, Ro,
Now five or six or so.
Riddle-me, Riddle-me, Ree,
Nine, ten crows round that tree.
Riddle-me, Riddle-me, Ro,
Now forty. He won't go.
Riddle-me, Riddle-me, Ree,
How deafening crows can be!
Riddle-me, Riddle-me, Ro,
The owl's still saying "No!"
Riddle-me, Riddle-me, Ree,
Did something leave the tree?
Riddle-me, Riddle-me, Ro,
You'll have to ask a crow.
Riddle-me, Riddle-me, Ree,
The crows are following he. . . .
Riddle-me, Riddle-me, Ro,
Are following *him*.

I know.

David McCord

RAT RIDDLES

There was a gray rat looked at me
with green eyes out of a rathole.

"Hello, rat," I said,
"Is there any chance for me
to get on to the language of the rats?"

And the green eyes blinked at me,
blinked from a gray rat's rathole.

"Come again," I said,
"Slip me a couple of riddles;
there must be riddles among the rats."

And the green eyes blinked at me
and a whisper came from the gray rathole:
"Who do you think you are and why is a rat?
Where did you sleep last night and why do you sneeze
    on Tuesdays? And why is the grave of a rat no
    deeper than the grave of a man?"

And the tail of a green-eyed rat
Whipped and was gone at a gray rathole.

Carl Sandburg

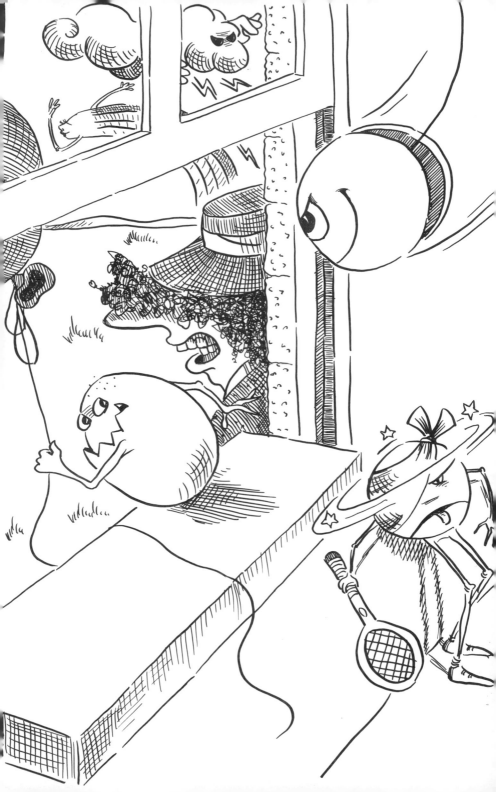

II. In or Out, Up or Down

Humpty Dumpty sat on a wall,	*Mother Goose*
I'm banged and chopped and sliced	*Lillian Morrison*
This Man Lives at My House Now	*John Ciardi*
Riddle me, riddle me, what is that,	*Anonymous*
I washed my face in water	*Anonymous*
Who?	*Riddle from India*
As soft as silk, as white as milk,	*Anonymous*
A milk-white bird	*Anonymous*
I Met a Man That Was All Head	*John Ciardi*
I never speak a word	*Mary Austin*
Black we are but much admired,	*Anonymous*
Voiceless it cries,	*J. R. R. Tolkien*
I come more softly than a bird,	*Mary Austin*
Who Am I?	*Riddle from India*

Humpty Dumpty sat on a wall,
Humpty Dumpty had a great fall.
  All the king's horses,
  And all the king's men,
Couldn't put Humpty together again.

Mother Goose

I'm banged and chopped and sliced
and severely beaten on
and then I am disowned
because my fuzz is gone.

Lillian Morrison

a tennis ball

THIS MAN LIVES AT MY HOUSE NOW

I met a man on my way to town.
He was spinning up, he was spinning down.
He was twice as red as the nose of a clown.

He took my hand as soon as we met,
And he said to me: "Now don't forget:
I'll spin and I'll spin and I'll spin for you.
I'll spin as fast as you want me to.
For I can spin up and I can spin down.
I can spin all the way to town."

And that's what he did till I told him to stop.
Can you guess his name?
                    —Is it MR. TOP?
He's a good spinner.
                    —Well, yes, so-so.
But he can't spin up and down. Oh no.
The man I met is called—MR. YOYO!

John Ciardi

Riddle me, riddle me, what is that,
Over the head, and under the hat?

Anonymous

hair

I washed my face in water
That neither rained nor run;
I dried my face on a towel
That was neither wove nor spun.

Anonymous

WHO?

Who whistled at my window?
Who stroked and smoothed my gown?
Who brought the scent of flowers?
Who knocked their petals down?

Who shook the yellow mango?
Who dropped it from its tree?
Who rattled all the branches?
Who tried to hide from me?

Riddle from India
translated by Sylvia Cassedy

the wind

As soft as silk, as white as milk,
As bitter as gall, a thick green wall,
And a brown coat covers me all.

Anonymous

a walnut

A milk-white bird
Floats down through the air.
And never a tree
But he lights there.

Anonymous

I MET A MAN THAT WAS ALL HEAD

I met a man that was all head.
He was fat as the moon but redder than red.
He had no ears. He had no chin.
And the rest of him was so long and thin
That it looked to me like nothing but string.

—You're making it up. There isn't a thing
As thin as that!
               —Yes, there is so.
He was out by the roses. I saw him go
Strolling along with his head held high,
And he nodded to me as he went by.
So I asked his name when I saw him stop
To smell a rose. And he said—POP!

—Well, where did he go? He isn't there.
And he couldn't just sink into thin air!

—Oh, yes he could! as you may see
If you guess his name. What could it be?
I'll give you three hints: he was fat as the moon,
And red as a yoyo, and bright as a spoon.
Now do you know? He was MR. BALLOON!

John Ciardi

I never speak a word
But when my voice is heard
Even the mountains shake,
No hands I have
And yet great rocks I break.

Mary Austin

thunder and lightning

Black we are but much admired,
Men seek for us till they are tired.
We tire horse, but comfort man.
Tell me this riddle, if you can.

Anonymous

coal

Voiceless it cries,
Wingless flutters,
Toothless bites,
Mouthless mutters.

J. R. R. Tolkien

the wind

I come more softly than a bird,
And lovely as a flower;
I sometimes last from year to year
And sometimes but an hour.

I stop the swiftest railroad train
Or break the stoutest tree.
And yet I am afraid of fire
And children play with me.

Mary Austin

WHO AM I?

My father is the Sun-God,
my mother is the sea;
My house is in the heavens,
the moonbeams play with me.

My gown has seven colors,
my song has seven keys;
I run among the mountains,
I bathe within the seas.

The world is ever waiting
for the little tinkling cry
of the bangles on my ankles
as I leap across the sky.

Riddle from India
translated by Sylvia Cassedy

a rainbow

III. Mostly Inside

There is one that has a head without an eye,
    And there's one that has an eye without a head:
You may find the answer if you try;
    And when all is said,
Half the answer hangs upon a thread.

Christina Rossetti

In marble halls as white as milk,
Lined with a skin as soft as silk,
Within a fountain crystal-clear,
A golden apple doth appear.
No doors there are to this stronghold,
Yet thieves break in and steal the gold.

Mother Goose

THE STRANGE TEETH

Forty teeth have I complete,
Yet I've never learned to eat;
Sometimes black and sometimes white,
Yet I cannot even bite!

Nancy Birckhead

a comb

WHAT AM I?

They chose me from my brothers:
    "That's the
Nicest one," they said,
And they carved me out a face and
     put a
Candle in my head;

And they set me on the doorstep. Oh,
    the
Night was dark and wild;
But when they lit the candle, then I
Smiled!

Dorothy Aldis

jack-o'-lantern

Little Nancy Etticoat,
With a white petticoat,
And a red nose;
She has no feet or hands,
The longer she stands
The shorter she grows.

Mother Goose

I've seen you where you never was,
And where you ne'er will be;
And yet you in that very same place
May still be seen by me.

Anonymous

face in a mirror

FROM A RIDDLE
(*for* Ponge)

It is always handled
with a certain

caution. After all,
it is present

on so many private
occasions. It goes

into all our darkest
corners. It accepts

a continual
diminution of itself

in the act
of moving, receiving

only a touch
in return. If a girl

lays it along
her cheek, it eases

the conscience. It salves
the raw wound

nipping it clean. To be
so mobile

and miss nothing
it has to be

soft. It is.

George Macbeth

deos

What's in a song, but not in a tune?
What's in a star, but not in the moon?
What's in the sun, but gone in the night,
Out of range, but still in sight?

J. Patrick Lewis

the letter s

FIVE SCOTTISH RIDDLE RHYMES

1.

Come a riddle, come a riddle,
Come a rote-tote-tote;
A wee, wee man, in a red, red coat,
A staff in his hand, and a bone in his throat;
Come a riddle, come a riddle,
Come a rote-tote-tote.

2.

What sits by your bed at night,
Gaping for your bones?
What gets up at morning light,
And clatters over the stones?

3.

I went and I got it.
I sat and I sought it.
And when I couldn't find it,
I brought it home.

4.

What is it that hangs high,
Cries through the air,
Has a head
And no hair?

5.

There's a wee, wee house,
And it's full of meat;
But neither door nor window
Will let you in to eat.

Adapted by Myra Cohn Livingston

1. a cherry 2. shoes 3. a thorn in the foot 4. a bell 5. an egg

Look me straight in the eye, I look straight back,
And I become everyone in the hall;
But turn on me then and scratch my back
And I am no one, no one at all.

William Jay Smith

a mirror.

To folks in Maine
    They're red and round,
And you can find them
    Underground.

In Idaho
    They're brown and big,
But still grow under-
    Ground. You dig?

                    J. Patrick Lewis

IV. Mostly Outside

An everywhere of silver,	*Emily Dickinson*
Tall and thin and topped with a T,	*William Jay Smith*
Runs all day and never walks,	*Mother Goose*
Whose	*Brian Swann*
Puzzle	*Robert Froman*
From Seven Natural Songs	*May Swenson*
Lives in winter,	*Mother Goose*
From Seven Natural Songs	*May Swenson*
Which tree can hang	*J. Patrick Lewis*
As white as milk,	*Wilhelmina Seegmiller*
Solo, you go	*Anita Wintz*
Who Cast My Shadow?	*Lilian Moore*
Drab habitation of whom?	*Emily Dickinson*

An everywhere of silver,
With ropes of sand
To keep it from effacing
The track called land.

Emily Dickinson

Tall and thin and topped with a T,
With trailing hair for all to see,
We do not speak but carry sound
Along the road for miles around.

William Jay Smith

Runs all day and never walks,
Often murmurs, never talks.
It has a bed, but never sleeps,
It has a mouth, but never eats.

Mother Goose

a river

WHOSE

Whose is that face?
At a wind's finger
it is broken and adrift

It is my face

It is my face I jump into
and fall through
I open my eyes
in a sleep of green
The horizon is over my head

till my crown bursts through
and my face takes in
as for the first time
the sky the poplars and the bright air

Brian Swann

PUZZLE

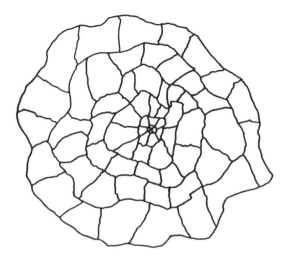

Map of city with streets meeting at center?

Net to catch people jumping from a burning building?

Spider's web?

Burner on an electric stove?

Fingerprint?

No.

Frozen puddle after a hit by a rock.

Robert Froman

FROM SEVEN NATURAL SONGS

Stood wooden, wiggled in earth way under.
A toenail scraped a mammoth's tusk.
Jounced and jittered all these lippy leaves.

May Swenson

Lives in winter,
Dies in summer.
And grows with its roots upward!

Mother Goose

an icicle

FROM SEVEN NATURAL SONGS

Slicked along meddling with rocks. Tore
their ears off gradually. Sparkling made
them hop and holler down a slate-cold throat.

May Swenson

Which tree can hang
  Along a lake,
Whose branches bend
  But will not break,

Whose leaves, sun-summered
  Into bloom,
Can whisk the water
  Like a broom?

Which tree will sigh
  As ripples pass
Across the crystal
  Looking glass,

Then lean beyond
  The shore's long shelf,
Reflecting sadly
  On itself?

J. Patrick Lewis

weeping willow

As white as milk,
As soft as silk,
And hundreds close together;
They sail away
On an autumn day,
When windy is the weather.

Wilhelmina Seegmiller

Solo, you go
rolling over and over
blown by the wind
scouring the valley
as if it were
a frying pan.

Anita Wintz

WHO CAST MY SHADOW?

I.

I'm lumpish,
plumpish,
your cheerful friend.
To my distress
I'm thinning,
beginning
my tearful end.
So hurry and guess.

II.

Did an artist weave my
shadow?
So finely made am I.
My silken lines spin
orb designs—
and peril to the fly.

III.

A shadow bird,
I fly
Between the earth and
sky.
Great in wing and
tail
How free I seem to sail!
Not so.
I cannot even move
till someone makes me go.

Lilian Moore

I. a snowman   II. a spider's web   III. an airplane

Drab habitation of whom?
Tabernacle or tomb,
Or dome of worm,
Or porch of gnome,
Or some elf's catacomb?

Emily Dickinson

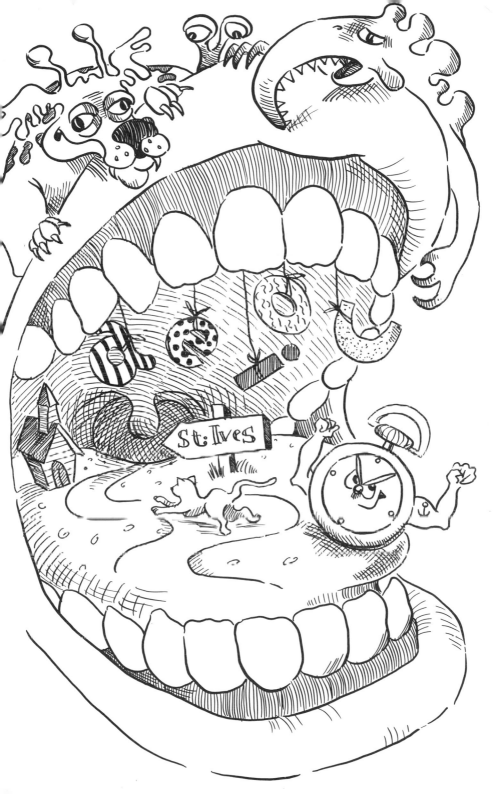

V. A Mixed Bag

RIDDLE

In the dripping gloom I see
A creature with broad antlers,
Motionless. It turns its head;
One gleaming eye devours the dark.
I hear it cough and clear its throat;
Then, with a hungry roar, it charges into the night
And is swallowed whole.

Ian Serraillier

a motorcycle

As I was going to Saint Ives,
I met a man with seven wives,
Each wife had seven sacks,
Each sack had seven cats,
Each cat had seven kits:
Kits, cats, sacks, and wives,
How many were there going to Saint Ives?

Mother Goose

This thing all things devours:
Birds, beasts, trees, flowers;
Gnaws iron, bites steel;
Grinds hard stones to meal;
Slays king, ruins town,
And beats high mountain down.

J. R. R. Tolkien

The beginning of eternity,
The end of time and space,
The beginning of every end,
The end of every place.

Anonymous

A worthless article
when it is all alone.
It only lives attached
to something of its own.
Russians never use it.
We wouldn't want to lose it.

Lillian Morrison

As I was going o'er Westminster bridge,
  I met with a Westminster scholar;
He pulled off his cap, *an' drew* off his glove,
  And wished me a very good morrow.

What is his name?

Anonymous

Andrew

There was a girl in our town,
Silk an' satin was her gown,
Silk an' satin, gold an' velvet,
Guess her name—three times I've tell'd it.

Anonymous

Ann

THE FIVE

We are little airy creatures,
All of different voice and features.
One of us in glass is set;
One of us you'll find in jet;
T'other you may see in tin;
And the fourth a box within;
If the fifth you should pursue,
It can never fly from you.

Jonathan Swift

the vowels: a e i o u

Thirty white horses
Upon a red hill,
Now they tramp,
Now they champ,
Now they stand still.

Mother Goose

teeth and gums

What's in the church
But not the steeple?
The parson has it,
But not the people.

Anonymous

RIDDLE

What do you do when you're up in a tree
And start to climb higher, when what do you see
But a Snaggletooth Scratch with a wart on its nose,
And a growl in its throat, and claws on its toes
Just waiting up there and looking at you,
Well, maybe, for nothing better to do,
And just licking its chops to pass the time?
Well, maybe. But anyway, back you climb.
And as soon as you're sitting safe on a branch
You happen to see a Hooknose Granch
Taking the view from the end of a limb.
And the view it is taking is, mostly dim.
And, mostly, of you. And full of hooks,
And clacking beaks, and hungry looks.
So you start to climb higher. And what do you see
But the snout of a Snarling Shivaree
With its forked tongue out, all drooly and twitchy,
And its nose wrinkled up as if it were itchy,
And a claw reaching down?—and you understand
It isn't trying to hold your hand
And invite you to pass the time of day,
And hope you feel you would like to stay
To be lunch, or dinner, or just a snack?
—Well, you can't climb up, and you can't climb back.
So now for the riddle: what do you do?

Give up? Yes, I think I would, too.

John Ciardi

VI. And Some with Answers

THE PRISONER

He cannot know
the day from night—
no window lets
a crack of light
into his prison,
bare and white.

No room to walk,
no room to crawl,
he lies there
curled up in a ball
and hangs his head
against the wall.

It breaks!
He falls out
in a heap.
He stands up, shakes,
and calls out
"Peep!"

Alice Schertle

a chick

Something's in my pocket,
What do you think?
It's nothing that goes down
The kitchen sink.

It isn't a penny,
It isn't a nail,
It isn't a cookie
That's nice and stale.

It isn't a whistle,
It isn't a stamp,
It isn't a toad
That's nice and damp.

It isn't an eraser
Or a ticket stub,
It isn't a piece
Of pocket flub.

It isn't a ring
Or string
Or a stone,
It isn't a bead
Or a weed
Or a bone.
I won't give it to you—
Get a hole of your own.

Eve Merriam

SPELLS

I dance and dance without any feet—
This is the spell of the ripening wheat.

With never a tongue I've a tale to tell—
This is the meadow-grasses' spell.

I give you health without any fee—
This is the spell of the apple-tree.

I rhyme and riddle without any book—
This is the spell of the bubbling brook.

Without any legs I run forever—
This is the spell of the mighty river.

I fall for ever and not at all—
This is the spell of the waterfall.

Without a voice I roar aloud—
This is the spell of the thunder-cloud.

No button or seam has my white coat—
This is the spell of the leaping goat.

I can cheat strangers with never a word—
This is the spell of the cuckoo bird.

We have tongues in plenty but speak no names—
This is the spell of the fiery flames.

The creaking door has a spell to riddle—
I play a tune without any fiddle.

James Reeves

PUZZLES FROM WONDERLAND

I.

Dreaming of apples on a wall,
    And dreaming often, dear,
I dreamed that if I counted all,
    How many would appear?

II.

A stick I found, that weighed two pound:
    I sawed it up one day
In pieces eight, of equal weight.
    How much did each piece weigh?

(Everybody says "a quarter of a pound" which is wrong.)

III.

John gave his brother James a box:
About it there were many locks.

James woke, and said it gave him pain;
So gave it back to John again.

This box was not with lid supplied,
Yet caused two lids to open wide:

And all these locks had never a key—
What kind of box, then, could it be?

IV.

What is most like a bee in May?
"Well, let me think: perhaps—" you say.
Bravo! You're guessing well to-day!

V.

Three sisters at breakfast were feeding the cat.
The first gave it sole—Puss was grateful for that:
The next gave it salmon—which Puss thought a treat:
The third gave it herring—which Puss wouldn't eat.

(Explain the conduct of the cat.)

VI.

Said the Moon to the Sun,
  "Is the daylight begun?"
Said the Sun to the Moon,
  "Not a minute too soon."

"You're a Full Moon," said he.
  She replied with a frown,
"Well! I never *did* see
  So uncivil a clown!"

(Query: *Why was the moon so angry?*)

VII.

When the King found that his money was nearly
gone, and that he really *must* live more economically, he
decided on sending away most of his Wise Men. There
were some hundreds of them—very fine old men, and
magnificently dressed in green velvet gowns with gold
buttons: if they *had* a fault, it was that they always
contradicted one another when he asked for their
advice—and they certainly ate and drank *enormously.* So,
on the whole, he was rather glad to get rid of them. But
there was an old law, which he did not dare to disobey,
which said that there must always be

  "Seven blind of both eyes:
    Ten blind of one eye:
  Five that see with both eyes:
    Nine that see with one eye."

(Query: *How many did he keep?*)

Solutions to Puzzles from Wonderland

I.   If ten the number dreamed of, why 'tis clear
     That in the dream ten apples would appear.

II. In Shylock's bargain for the flesh, was found
     No mention of the blood that flowed around;
     So when the stick was sawed in pieces eight,
     The sawdust lost diminished from the weight.

III. As curly-wigg'd Jemmy was sleeping in bed
     His brother John gave him a blow on the head;

James opened his eyelids, and spying his brother,
Doubled his fist, and gave him another.
This kind of box then is not so rare;
The lids are the eyelids, the locks are the hair;
And as every schoolboy can tell to his cost,
The key to the tangles is constantly lost.

IV.   'Twixt "Perhaps" and "May be"
Little difference we see:
Let the question go round,
the Answer is found.

V.   The salmon and sole Puss should think very grand
Is no such remarkable thing,
For more of these dainties Puss took up her stand:
But when the third sister stretched out her fair hand
Pray why should Puss swallow her ring?

VI.   "In these degenerate days," we oft hear said,
"Manners are lost, and chivalry dead!"
No wonder since in high exalted spheres
The same degeneracy, in fact, appears.

The Moon in social matters interfering,
Scolded the Sun, when early in appearing;
And the rude Sun, her gentle sex ignoring,
Called her a fool, thus her pretensions flooring.

VII.   Five seeing, and seven blind,
Give us twelve in all, we find;
But all of these, 'tis very plain,
Come into account again.
For take notice, it may be true,
That those blind of one eye are blind of two;
And consider contrariwise,
That to see with your eye you may have your eyes;
So setting one against the other—
For a mathematician no great bother—
And working the sum, you will understand
That sixteen wise men still trouble the land.

Eadgyth
(Lewis Carroll)

IT ISN'T

It isn't a bud
that turns into a rose,
but it grows.

It isn't a set
of musical bells,
but it yells.

It isn't a hippo
with triple chins,
but it grins.

It isn't a goat
eating paper bags,
but it na-aa-ags.

It isn't a vine
wrapped 'round a tree,
but it trails after me.

It's no other
than
my baby brother.

Eve Merriam

Oh send to me an apple that hasn't any kernel,
And send to me a capon without a bone or feather,
And send to me a ring that has no twist or circlet,
And send to me a baby that's all grace and good temper.

How could there be an apple that hasn't any kernel?
How could there be a capon without a bone or feather?
How could there be a ring that has no twist or circlet?
How could there be a baby that's all grace and good
    temper?

The apple in its blossom hadn't any kernel;
And when the hen was sitting there was no bone or
    feather;
And when the ring was melting it had no twist or circlet;
And when we were in love there was grace and good
    temper.

Anonymous
translated from the Welsh
by Gwyn Williams

MINGLED YARNS

What stories are mixed together?

1. Whose cherry tree did young George chop?
   It was Pinocchio's
   And every time George told a lie
   He grew an inch of nose.

2. Jack be nimble,
   Jack be quick,
   Jack jump over
   The beanstalk stick!

3. Aladdin had a little lamp,
   It smelled all keroseny.
   And everywhere Aladdin took
   His lamp jam-packed with genii.

   He took his lamp to school one day,
   Which made the teacher blubber
   And all the children laugh to see
   Young Al the old lamp-rubber.

   X. J. Kennedy

THE RIDDLING KNIGHT

There were three sisters fair and bright,
  Jennifer, Gentle and Rosemary,
And they three loved one valiant knight—
  As the dow* flies over the mulberry-tree.

The eldest sister let him in,
And barr'd the door with a silver pin.

The second sister made his bed,
And placed soft pillows under his head.

The youngest sister that same night
Was resolved for to wed wi' this valiant knight.

"And if you can answer questions three,
O then, fair maid, I'll marry wi' thee.

"O what is louder nor a horn,
Or what is sharper nor a thorn?

"Or what is heavier nor the lead,
Or what is better nor the bread?

"Or what is longer nor the way,
Or what is deeper nor the sea?"

"O shame is louder nor a horn,
And hunger is sharper nor a thorn.

"O sin is heavier nor the lead,
The blessing's better nor the bread.

"O the wind is longer nor the way
And love is deeper nor the sea."

"You have answer'd aright my questions three,"
  Jennifer, Gentle and Rosemary;
"And now, fair maid, I'll marry wi' thee,"
  As the dow flies over the mulberry-tree.

Anonymous

*dove

RIDDLE

In the middle of
  the middle of
  the middle
  grows a horn!

It's a riddle of
  a riddle of
  a riddle—
  Who is born

  with a little white horse body?
  a beard just like a goat?
  a lion's tail—and hind legs
  like a graceful antelope?

  a horn that spirals upwards
  from the middle of his head
  (which begins in white and then turns black
  and finally ends up red)?

In the middle of
  the middle of
  his forehead grows a horn

And the answer
  to the riddle is
  a wondrous unicorn!

Myra Cohn Livingston

RIDDLES WISELY EXPOUNDED or THE DEVIL'S TEN QUESTIONS

If you don't answer my questions well,
   Sing ninety-nine and ninety,
I'll take you off, and I live in Hell,
   And you the weavering bonty.

Oh, what is whiter far than milk?
   Sing ninety-nine and ninety!
And what is softer far than silk?
   And you the weavering bonty!

Oh, snow is whiter far than milk,
   Sing ninety-nine and ninety!
And down is softer far than silk,
   And me the weavering bonty!

Oh, what is louder than a horn?
   Sing ninety-nine and ninety!
And what is sharper than a thorn?
   And you the weavering bonty!

Oh, thunder's louder than a horn,
   Sing ninety-nine and ninety!
And death is sharper than a thorn,
   And me the weavering bonty!

Oh, what is higher than a tree?
   Sing ninety-nine and ninety!
And what is deeper than the sea?
   And you the weavering bonty!

Oh, Heaven's higher than a tree,
   Sing ninety-nine and ninety!
And Hell is deeper than the sea,
   And me the weavering bonty!

Oh, what red fruit September grows?
  Sing ninety-nine and ninety!
And what thing round the whole world goes?
  And you the weavering bonty!

The apple in September grows,
  Sing ninety-nine and ninety!
And the air around the whole world goes,
  And me the weavering bonty!

Oh, what is wicked man's repay?
  Sing ninety-nine and ninety!
And what is worse than woman's way?
  And you the weavering bonty!

Now Hell is wicked man's repay,
  Sing ninety-nine and ninety!
And a she-devil's worse than woman's way,
  And me the weavering bonty!

Oh, you have answered my question well,
  Sing ninety-nine and ninety!
But I'll take you off, 'cause I live in Hell,
  And you the weavering bonty!

Traditional: American

RIDDLE-GO-ROUND

Riddle go round and roundabout.
Is the middle of a wood
halfway in
or halfway out?

The farther in,
the nearer out?
Riddle go round and roundabout,
are you sure
or do you doubt?

Maybe so,
maybe no,
riddle go round and roundabout,
how to find the way to go?

Haps perhaps stand your ground,
answer hasn't yet been found,
riddle go round and roundabout.

Riddle go round and roundabout
ask your father
ask your mother
ask your little
baby brother.

Halfway out
or halfway in,
guess it right
and you can win.

Dilly dally
shilly shally
is the middle of a wood
halfway in
or halfway out?

Haps perhaps stand your ground,
answer hasn't yet been found,
riddle go round and round and round
and round and round and round.

Eve Merriam

INDEX OF AUTHORS AND TRANSLATORS

INDEX OF TITLES

INDEX OF FIRST LINES

In the middle of   81
It is always handled   37
It isn't a bud   77
I've seen you where you never was,   36

Jack be nimble,   79
John gave his brother James a box: 74

Little Nancy Etticoat,   35
Lives in winter,   50
Look me straight in the eye, I look straight back,   40

Map of city with streets meeting at center?   48
My body a rounded stone   10
My father is the Sun-God,   28

Oh send to me an apple that hasn't any kernel,   78

Riddle go round and roundabout,   84
Riddle me, riddle me, what is that,   19
Riddle-me, Riddle-me, Ree,   12
Runs all day and never walks,   46

Said the Moon to the Sun,   75
Slicked along meddling with rocks. Tore   51
Solo, you go   54
Something's in my pocket,   72
Stood wooden, wiggled in earth way under.   49

Tall and thin and topped with a T,   45
The beginning of eternity,   62
There is one that has a head without an eye,   31
There was a girl in our town,   64
There was a gray rat looked at me   13
There were three sisters fair and bright,   80
There's a wee, wee house,   39
They chose me from my brothers: 34
Thirty white horses   66
This thing all things devours: 61
Three sisters at breakfast were feeding the cat.   74
To folks in Maine   41

Voiceless it cries,   26

We are little airy creatures,   65